KING FLASHYPANTS

AND THE EVIL EMPEROR

KiNG FLASHYPANTS

AND THE EVIL EMPEROR

BOOK 1

WRITTEN AND DRAWN BY **ANDY RILEY**

Henry Holt and Company • New York

Henry Holt and Company, *Publishers since 1866*
Henry Holt® is a registered trademark of Macmillan Publishing Group, LLC.
175 Fifth Avenue, New York, New York 10010 • mackids.com

Library of Congress Cataloging-in-Publication Data
Names: Riley, Andy, author, illustrator.
Title: King Flashypants and the evil emperor / Andy Riley.
Description: First American edition. | New York : Henry Holt and Company, 2017. |
First published in 2016. | Summary: Nine-year-old King Edwin is
loved by his people, but when he runs out of money evil Emperor Nurbison
sees it as a chance to seize control of Edwinland.
Identifiers: LCCN 2016035890 (print) | LCCN 2017012802 (ebook) |
ISBN 9781627798099 (hardcover) | ISBN 9781627798105 (ebook)
Subjects: | CYAC: Kings, queens, rulers, etc.—Fiction. |
Money—Fiction. | Generosity—Fiction. | Humorous stories.
Classification: LCC PZ7.1.R547 Kin 2017 (print) |
LCC PZ7.1.R547 (ebook) | DDC [Fic]—dc23
LC record available at https://lccn.loc.gov/2016035890

Our books may be purchased in bulk for promotional, educational,
or business use. Please contact your local bookseller or the Macmillan
Corporate and Premium Sales Department at (800) 221-7945 ext. 5442
or by e-mail at MacmillanSpecialMarkets@Macmillan.com

Originally published in 2016 in Great Britain by Hodder and Stoughton
First American edition—2017 / Design by Jennifer Stephenson
Printed in the United States of America by LSC Communications,
Harrisonburg, Virginia

1   3   5   7   9   10   8   6   4   2

For Polly, Eddie, and Bill

With thanks to
Emma Goldhawk, Jennifer Stephenson,
Anne McNeil, Gordon Wise,
Hilary Murray Hill, and Kevin Cecil

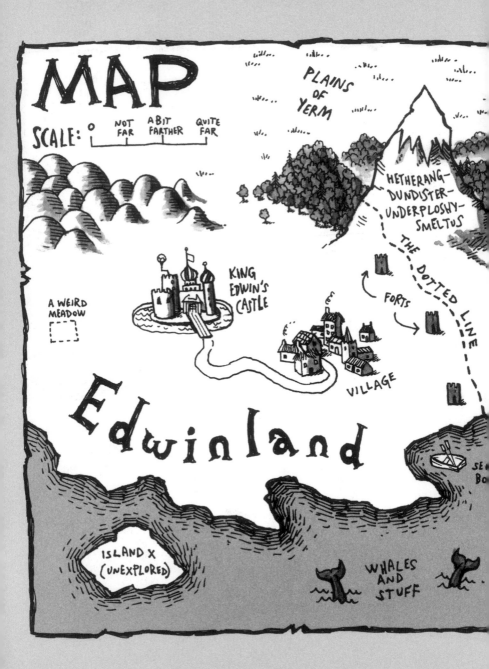

KING EDWIN

MEGAN THE JESTER

MINISTER JILL

EMPEROR
NURBISON

GLOBULUS

The Names of ALL THE THRILLING CHAPTERS You're About to Read

Pocket Money

"I'd like my pocket money now, please," said the boy, and in came a man with a wheelbarrow brimming with gold coins.

Edwin wasn't an ordinary nine-year-old boy. He was a king, with a throne and his own suit of armor and a castle with secret passages and everything. Best of all, he had a crown.

A crown is very important. If he didn't have one, you would just say, "Look at that boy over there. Doesn't he look amazingly normal, like any other kid?" But put a crown on his head and you say, "Wow! He's a boy *and* he's a king! I bet he has fun and lots of adventures. What's a king without a crown?"

This crown was really special because each point had a little crown on the top. The crown had crowns. You can't get more crowny than that. No wonder King Edwin never took it off.

"Thank you very much," said Edwin to the palace guard with the wheelbarrow, because even though he was the ruler, he was a very polite boy.

King Edwin delved into the gold and pulled out a great, gleaming handful. All the coins had his face on one side. He always got a buzz out of that.

Edwin turned to his special helper. "I'm leaving the castle for a bit, Jill!" he said.

. . . Minister Jill said while writing two letters at once, one with each hand. Try it sometime. It's not easy.

Jill was always busy. Jill was a grown-up with a very grown-up job. Even though Edwin was the ruler of the kingdom of Edwinland, he needed an adult to help him with the complicated parts.

Who had to find a dancing bear for a birthday feast? Jill.

Who had to write a letter of apology when the dancing bear ate somebody's arm? Jill.

Jill worked as much as Edwin played, and Edwin played a lot.

Edwin trundled the coin-filled wheelbarrow down a lane.

"Afternoon!" said King Edwin.

"Afternoon, Your Majesty!" said a passing peasant.

Edwin's kingdom had peasants, but they weren't miserable, hungry peasants dressed in sacks and boiling nettles for dinner. No, these were *merry* peasants, all plump and smiling. Whenever the day's work was done, they danced in the town square for the sheer joy of being alive.

Edwin headed for the nearest village. Edwinland wasn't a big country, so there was only one. It was called "Village." If they ever built a second village, then Village would be in serious need of renaming.

King Edwin went into a candy shop. There were a lot of candy shops in Village. He grabbed two heavy fistfuls of gold coins and spilled them across the counter.

"Hello. I'd like every chocolate, every chocolate bar, and every chocolate-based snack in this shop."

"The usual order, Your Majesty? Certainly."

Minutes later, King Edwin left the shop with a huge mound of goodies in his wheelbarrow.

Then he bought everything in the next candy shop.

And the next.

And the next.

By half past five, Edwin was balancing
an enormous, wobbling tower of chocolate
in his wheelbarrow. He tipped it into a
giant funnel attached to a pipe, attached
to a wheel, attached to another pipe,
attached to a piston, attached to . . . well,

you get the idea. It was quite a complicated machine: King Edwin's Nutritious Nibbles Ejector, Thrower, and Hurler. Or K.E.N.N.E.T.H. for short.

The king rode K.E.N.N.E.T.H. through the streets of Village, spraying chocolate in every direction. The peasants ran out of their houses, grabbing all they could. It was their favorite part of the week.

"It's a powerful, good king we have in this land," the peasants would say.

"Spends all his pocket money on us, he does!"

"Yes. Because he loves us."

And they loved him right back. Some weeks they loved him so much they would declare Friday to be We Love the King Day, and everybody would celebrate instead of going to work or school. If it went really well, Monday would be a We Love the King Day, too.

On those days, Minister Jill would mumble things like "lazy peasants" and "any excuse" under her breath, but Edwin didn't think she

was being fair. The people loved the king, the king loved the people, they *all* loved chocolate, and that was that.

The next Friday, as Edwin sat on his throne waiting for his pocket money to arrive, he thought to himself, *This isn't a bad life. I'm a lucky boy. In fact, I'm so lucky, I bet nothing will go wrong for me ever again.*

The palace guard pushed the wheelbarrow into the throne room.

Edwin stared.

The wheelbarrow was empty.

"Your Majesty? The money's all gone."

Foo Hoo Hoo Hoo

A tall figure rose from a dark and spiky throne.

"GUARDS? SEIZE HIM!" said the figure.

The sinister soldiers looked around, confused. There was nobody to seize. Emperor Nurbison slumped back into his throne. He knew there was no one about, but he just liked shouting "GUARDS? SEIZE HIM!" whenever he felt like it. And that was quite a lot.

There are plenty of ways to tell if an emperor is an evil emperor. First, take a good look at his castle, most likely as you are taken toward it in a cage on the back of a wagon.

The castle of a good king is made of warm-colored stone. Yellow or light brown. The whole thing is always wider than it is tall, and there is a brightly colored flag on the top. Edwin's castle was just like that.

The castle of an evil emperor looks totally different. It's always taller than it is wide. It's made of jagged black stone, and it stands on a tall, jagged rock. You can only get to it by a steep, windy path with no hand rails. Evil emperors never care about health and safety.

Nurbison's castle was just like that. Only his was extra super evil because it was surrounded on all sides by a bottomless pit. Bottomless pits are very rare. Probably because they take a very long time to dig.

He wore a black cloak, black tights, black boots, and a little goatee beard. To top it all off, his evil crown bristled with sharp spikes, and it didn't glitter at all. In place of twinkly diamonds, he had priceless anti-diamonds that sucked light in and kept it there.

DIAMOND   ANTI-DIAMOND

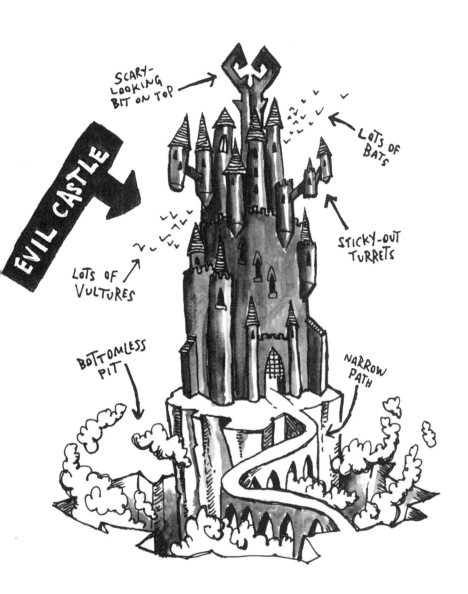

SCARY-LOOKING BIT ON TOP

EVIL CASTLE

LOTS OF BATS

STICKY-OUT TURRETS

LOTS OF VULTURES

BOTTOMLESS PIT

NARROW PATH

But his laugh set him apart from the rest of the evil crowd. "Bwahahahaha" had been done. So had "muhahahahaha." So Emperor Nurbison plumped for a spine-chilling

"FOO HOO HOO HOO HOO HOO."

Try it. It'll terrify everyone around you.

All the same, the emperor wasn't laughing very much that day. He hadn't done anything dastardly all morning. After breakfast, he had deliberately trapped a fly in the window's

double glazing

and let it

bump around

between

the two bits

of glass

for at least ten

minutes

before releasing it.

But that hardly

counted.

"Globulus!

The map!" said the

emperor.

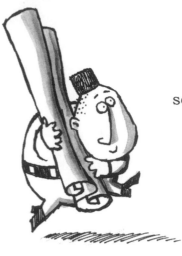

Globulus, the emperor's servant, came running in. He was the exact shape and size of a beach ball. He unrolled a map across a huge wooden table.

"See these many lands?" said Emperor Nurbison. "So many of them belong to me now. So, so many . . ."

Globulus pointed to the edge of the map.

"But not, kind of like, you know, Edwinland?"

"Edwinland!" spat the emperor as he jammed a dagger into the map (a great trick they teach you at evil

school). "Ruled by that moon-faced boy with that ridiculous shiny crown he loves so much. He's a proper little king flashypants. Somehow my sinister soldiers cannot defeat his palace guards. . . ."

He glared at the sinister soldiers. They shuffled a bit and looked at the floor.

"But soon!" Emperor Nurbison said. "Soon the day shall come when that foolish boy makes a fatal mistake. And then . . ."

Globulus and the sinister soldiers waited silently for the emperor to finish.

"And then . . . !"

Still everyone waited.

"AND THEN . . . Well, Globulus? Get the bowl!"

"Oh! Yes, Your Majesty!"

Globulus ran out of the throne room and rushed back a few seconds later with a bowl of fruit.

"As I was saying . . . And then I will crush Edwinland as easily as I crush this fruit!"

Emperor Nurbison grabbed a grape and
got crushing. Juice ran down his arm.

"FOO HOO HOO HOO HOO. FOO HOO HOO HOO HOO!"

said the emperor. "Come on, join in, everybody!

FOO HOO HOO HOO HOO!"

Globulus and the sinister soldiers did the laugh. Not quite as scarily as Emperor Nurbison, though. The emperor didn't like it if you did anything better than him.

"Fetch my telescope," said the emperor. "I shall watch Edwin's kingdom. I shall watch and wait and make my plans against him!" And with a last "foo hoo hoo hoo," the emperor twirled his cloak and strode from the hall.

Pig

King Edwin and Minister Jill were climbing inside a pig. The pig didn't utter a single oink of complaint. It was made of china.

Kings don't have normal piggy banks. They have massive ones. The official piggy bank of Edwinland was as big as a house and stood in the middle of the castle courtyard.

Any visitor to the Great Pig had to climb through a slot high on its back. There was a much easier circular door in its belly, stopped with a big rubber plug, but you could only use that when you were leaving.

"Aaaaaaarrrrrgh!"

said Jill

as she

tumbled

through

the slot

and thumped

onto the

pottery floor.

"Aaaaaarrrrrgh!"

said Jill again
as King Edwin
landed on her,
pointy crown
first.

35

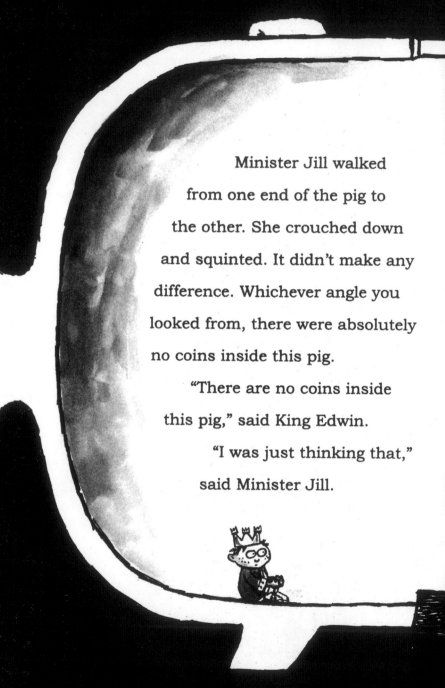

Minister Jill walked
from one end of the pig to
the other. She crouched down
and squinted. It didn't make any
difference. Whichever angle you
looked from, there were absolutely
no coins inside this pig.

"There are no coins inside
this pig," said King Edwin.

"I was just thinking that,"
said Minister Jill.

"So where have they all
gone, then?"

"Well," said Jill, "remember
how I put you in charge of the
kingdom's money? To give you
some practice running the kingdom
yourself when you're a grown-up?"

"You mean, when you let me
choose how much pocket
money I get? Yeah.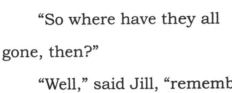
That was brilliant."

Minister Jill closed her eyes and pinched the top of her nose.

Ah, thought Edwin. *That's one of those things grown-ups do when they get stressed.*

Maybe Jill was stressed.

"You haven't been spending it all on chocolate, have you?" said Jill.

"No," said King Edwin.

"So what else, then?"

"I paid a carpenter to make a bigger wheelbarrow, to get more money from the Great Pig, so I could buy my peasants even more chocolate."

"Where do you think all the money comes from, Your Majesty?" said Jill.

"Hmmmm . . . ," said King Edwin, digging his finger into his ear while he tried to remember. "There's Uncle Gavin. He's a duke of somewhere or other. He always sends me a boatload of treasure on my birthday."

"No, he sends it when Duchess Karen *reminds* him it's your birthday. I don't think she reminded him this year."

"Oh. Right."

"So now the kingdom has no money. Remember that lesson I taught you a few months ago? Everything a king needs to know about money? I think we need to do it again."

King Edwin nodded. He knew Minister Jill was about to use lots of complicated grown-up words, and it would be very hard for any nine-year-old to concentrate.

I *will try to concentrate*, thought the king. *Nothing to distract me in this empty, pig-shaped room. Except a little bit of blue sky I can see through the slot at the top.*

?

?

?

?

?

Why is the **sky blue?**

Also, why is the **sea blue?**

Maybe because it's so full of **blue whales.**

?

ENORMOUS BLUE WHALES

from top to bottom.

If that were true, it would be pretty ?

hard for the whales, *he thought.*

?

They would **BASH** *into one another all the time.* ?

But maybe when they do, it makes a wave,

and that's where waves come from.

?

41

*I could be a **top scientist** as well as a **king** when I grow up*, thought Edwin. *I will design **crash helmets** for blue whales. **And then I will—"***

"Your Majesty? Your Majesty? Are you listening?"

"What? Yeah! Totally," said King Edwin, sitting up. "I just missed the last bit. Could you say that again?"

"So where should I start from?"

"Um—the beginning? Sorry."

"Try to concentrate this time," said Minister Jill. "A country gathers money through taxation and borrowing. . . ."

King Edwin felt his mind wandering
even quicker this time. Oh dear. *Think about
the boring stuff Jill's saying,* he thought to
himself. *Don't think about cool things like
whales or the sea. Think about dry land.*

King Edwin imagined he was looking at a big map of his own country. Then he thought,

if you're looking at a **map,**

and the place where you are right now is on it,

if you looked at that **exact spot** → •

on the map through a **microscope,**

you would see a tiny picture *of yourself.*

 And that tiny you *is looking at*

an absolutely minuscule **map.**

If you had an even more
powerful microscope,

you would see the even more tiny you

 that the tiny you is looking at.

And that tiny tiny you would be looking

at an amazingly small *map,*

with a tiny tiny tiny you who is looking at a

tiny tiny tiny tiny you and so on and so on. . . .

"YOUR MAJESTY!"

"Ah! Hello. What were you talking about again?" said the king.

Minister Jill took a deep breath. "The lesson will have to wait," she said. "The kingdom needs money right now. I know just where to look. Let's get out of this pig."

The king and the minister jumped up
and down on the big rubber stopper at the
bottom. It took a while to budge, but finally
it gave way, and the pair of them *thonk*ed
into the courtyard.

"Your Majesty, please summon the palace guards," said Minister Jill.

The king blew on a giant horn. Every stone in the castle shook. Doves fluttered into the air.

There were lots of ways to summon the palace guards, but the giant horn was definitely the coolest.

Soon the guards stood in front of King
Edwin, ten rows deep.
They were a
fearsome-looking
bunch. They
had to be, to
keep people
like Emperor
Nurbison out of
Edwinland.

"At Your
Majesty's service!"
said Centurion Alisha,
the commander of
the guards.

Alisha had a powerful stare. One glance from her could knock a nail into a piece of wood.

Minister Jill gave the orders. There were countless rooms in King Edwin's castle. Nobody knew how many for sure. Lots of those rooms had sofas. The guards had to stick their hands inside every sofa in the castle to see if there was any loose change hiding down there.

Off they went, plunging their arms into the furniture.

Some of them got their chain mail stuck on the sofa tassels, and it took another six guards to pull them free.

But they didn't find very much money.

"Call *all* the guards in the kingdom!" said Minister Jill. "Tell them to check every sofa five times!"

Centurion Alisha growled a command. The message went out across the countryside by horse, smoke signal, and tin cans on string. Before long, guards came running in from every fort in the land.

"It's going to be okay, isn't it?" asked King Edwin.

"Yes, yes, Your Majesty. It's all going to be fine," said Minister Jill.

The king wondered why, if it was all going to be fine, the minister had started chewing a strand of her own hair.

• • •

Far, far away, a hunched figure peered

through a telescope.

He saw Edwin's guards running from

their forts toward the young king's castle.

His evil lips parted.

The Coming of the Emperor

There was a dotted line painted on the ground.

Emperor Nurbison stood on one side of it. His big collar flapped in the wind, and the pointy bits jabbed other people in the eyes. But nobody was allowed to say "ouch" or

"aargh" or "For heaven's sake, get a less stupid coat."

The emperor took one step forward, over the line.

"And now I stand in Edwinland!" he said to Globulus and the sinister soldiers. "And where are his legendary palace guards? Are they here to throw me back into my own country? No! They are not!"

"'Cause yesterday all the guards, like, went running to his castle. I reckon there's some sort of emergency or something," said Globulus.

"Some sort of emergency or something," said the emperor. "A fine analysis of the situation, Globulus. Let us stride to the nearest village, and there we will learn if this emergency can help me."

Emperor Nurbison loved to have scary music playing as he strode. So a marching band walked along behind him, walloping big drums and blasting trumpets. They played "The Emperor's Striding Theme" and an even more terrifying song they'd been working on called

"ANTHEM OF DESTRUCTION."

It was quite a long walk to Village, so they played each tune three times, as well as "Twinkle, Twinkle, Little Star."

The emperor cast his eye down Village's

56

main street. Instead of the smiling, happy peasants he might have seen on any other day, he saw sad, worried-looking peasants.

"Peasant! Approach!" he said to one of them.

"Oh, hello," said the peasant. "Aren't you evil Emperor Nurbison, sworn enemy of happiness, and the eternal foe of King Edwin?"

"Why, yes, I am! Globulus, give him a signed picture."

Globulus handed the peasant a signed drawing of the emperor

standing on a big rock, looking into the

distance, with an eagle perched on his hand.

"Why has this become a land of

misery?" said the emperor. "I thought the

peasants here were of the merry sort?"

"Yesterday, the king didn't come to give us chocolate. He always does that on Fridays."

More peasants clustered round.

"None of us can handle a Friday without chocolate. That's too much for anyone."

"We love our king, but it's like he's . . ."

"It's like he's forgotten us!"

"We'd ask one of the guards what's going on, but there are none around. They're all at the palace."

The emperor nodded and frowned, as if he felt sorry for the peasants.

"This, like, situation here and stuff. You could, you know . . . do a thing," said Globulus.

"If by 'do a thing' you mean 'use their unhappiness to seize this land,' then yes, I could indeed 'do a thing.'"

Emperor Nurbison climbed onto a hay cart. They're very good for making big olden-day speeches on short notice.

"Workers! Peasants! Scum!" the evil emperor began. Then he remembered he needed to be nice to them, at least for the next hour or so.

"I mean . . . dear friends! If your king has not brought you chocolates and sweets, he has indeed forgotten you!"

There was a moan from the crowd.

"But fear not! All you need to do is rise up! Rise against the king who no longer loves you. Overthrow him, I say, and I, Emperor Nurbison, Earl of Unjerland, Overlord of Glenth and Boolander, Monarch of the Salty Marshes of Splop, shall be your new ruler!"

The peasants patiently watched the emperor for a while.

"That was the end of the speech," Nurbison said. "Honestly, I thought flapping my arms and shaking my finger at the sky would have given you a *bit* of a clue. Anyway, will you rise against King Edwin?"

The peasants sat in a circle and talked it over.

"Seems reasonable," said one peasant.

"Yes, I thought the emperor had a lot of interesting things to say," said another.

A very small peasant jumped into the middle of the circle. She was called Natasha, and she was seven years old.

"But he's an *evil* emperor," said Natasha. "So anything he says might be a lie."

Hardly anybody tells a lie in Edwinland, so the peasants had forgotten that not everywhere was like that.

"Powerful point," said another peasant.

"Food for thought," said another.

On they talked.

Emperor Nurbison leaned over to Globulus. "What exactly is going on here?"

"I reckon they're, you know, having different points of view and telling each other about them," Globulus replied.

"Oh. I've heard about this kind of thing.

It's called a 'discussion.' I certainly won't be letting that happen when I take over. But it's fascinating to see one going on."

The discussion went on and on. The emperor grew more and more impatient. He drummed his fingers on Globulus's head.

"They're not yet ready to turn against their king," Nurbison said to Globulus. "We need more . . . something big, to win them over."

"Sort of like, there's a curse on the kingdom? Something like that?"

"Exactly like that. Quickly, back to my castle!"

They all ran back to Nurbisonia. The band played "The Emperor's Striding Theme," but three times faster than normal.

Later that afternoon, Emperor Nurbison sat back on his throne and admired his work.

"The citizens of Edwinland will get rid of their puny king when they see their land has been cursed. And what better curse is there than a scary monster? Here is such a monster!

"Behold . . .

the

terrifying

dragon!"

Globulus and the sinister soldiers stared at the dragon.

Except it wasn't really a dragon. There hadn't been dragons in the world for hundreds of years. So the emperor had found a cow and spent the last two hours using his incredible crafting skills to make it look like a dragon.

Its wings were made from wire coat hangers and crepe paper. Its hooves were now claws—or rather, two pairs of furry-monster novelty slippers that the emperor had been given for his birthday but had never worn. The tail was a long sock stuffed with tissue paper. Two candles stuck on the cow's nose were the "fiery breath." The animal was painted green. Or at least the front half was—the paint had run out. The emperor had tried to color in the back half of the cow with felt-tip pens, but he had never been very good at putting the tops back on his felt tips, and they had all dried up. But the emperor thought it would be okay, because if the cow was scary enough in the front, the peasants would run away before they saw the back.

"We will let this fearsome dragon loose on the streets of Edwinland," said Emperor Nurbison. "We will tell them their kingdom is cursed until Edwin is gone. Soon!

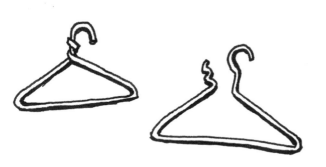

Soon I shall crush Edwinland as I crush this fruit!"

Globulus looked around the room. The fruit bowl had been taken away to make room for the emperor's craft box.

"As I crush this fruit . . . As I crush this . . . Oh, somebody get some! An apple! A fig! A cherry, I don't care!"

And Globulus ran from the room, a piece of crepe paper stuck to the back of his trousers.

#

King Edwin sat on his throne. He was
very sad. He loved his subjects more than
anything, and if he couldn't give them
presents of chocolate and sweets, he just
didn't know what to do with himself.

Minister Jill had told him there were
lots of other ways to show the peasants

he loved them that wouldn't cost so much money. "How about giving them homemade presents?" she'd said. Edwin had noticed how grown-ups always love to suggest that. When you give a grown-up a homemade present, they always say it's really good and better than anything you could get from the store, even when that's not true, which is most of the time.

Edwin needed something to cheer him up—and fast. So he did that double clap that kings do when they want attention.

In a far corner of the throne room, a jester-shaped door opened, and Megan the Jester ran out, bells tinkling. Megan was

Edwin's favorite person in the world because she was just so big and tall and funny.

"What amusements would you like, Your Majesty?" said Megan.

"Well, that falling-over thing you do is always brilliant. Can you do that?"

Megan skipped across the floor, tripped over a wonky stone slab, and fell flat on her face. Edwin roared with laughter—so she did it again. And again. Edwin kept on laughing. But after she had done it seventy or eighty times, the joke was starting to wear off.

King Edwin sighed. He was thinking about those poor, hungry peasants once more.

Megan got out a lute, which is a sort of olden-days guitar.

"I'll sing you a song, Your Majesty! This one's called 'My Very Nice Cat.'"

Megan played and sang.

I had a cat.

She had no tail,

no legs or paws

beneath her.

She had no

nose,

she had no

ears,

she had no whiskers,

either.

No neck,

no chest,

no head,

no claws.

No eyes had she to stare.

In fact, she didn't

exist at all,

she wasn't really there.

But she was my cat,

my very nice cat.

and I called her Valerie.

My cat, my

very nice cat.

dee dee, dee

dee, dee dee.

It was one of her better songs. By the time Megan got to the big lute solo, Edwin had forgotten all his troubles.

Just then, Minister Jill burst into the room.

"Your Majesty! The citizens are attacking the castle!"

King Edwin, Minister Jill, and Megan the Jester ran to the battlements. It was true. The peasants had risen. But they were apologizing for it.

"We're really sorry!" said the peasants as they pushed long ladders against the castle walls.

"We hope you're not too upset about this!" they said as they smashed against the great wooden door with a battering ram.

"We hope we can all still be friends!" they said as they hurled huge rocks at the building with a giant catapult.

"Why do you turn against your king?"

shouted Minister Jill. "You can survive one day without chocolate, can't you?"

"But there's the curse!" said a peasant. "An evil dragon came to burn our crops! He won't go until we have a new ruler!"

Little Natasha was following the rest of the peasants, bouncing up and down with rage.

"It's not a dragon!" she yelled. "It's a cow with candles on its nose! Anyone can see that! And it never set fire to the crops. It just tried to eat some grass and singed a dandelion." But her words were drowned out by the battering ram and the catapults.

Watching the whole thing from a nearby

hillock was the dastardly Emperor Nurbison, patting the cow that kind-of-sort-of looked like a dragon.

The emperor was too far from the castle for the king to hear a "FOO HOO HOO HOO," so Globulus held up a big sign for Edwin to read.

"So that bad, beardy man's behind this! I should have known," said King Edwin.

The castle door broke, and the peasants surged inside.

"We'll deal with him later," said Minister Jill. "First, let's defend the castle. Centurion Alisha? Stop the peasants from getting in!" said Minister Jill.

Alisha pulled out her big sword with a

sCHWWAAAAANG

sound. All the other guards did the same.

sCHWWAAAAANG.

sCHWWAAAAANG

sCHWWAAAAANG.

"Stop!" said King Edwin. "I don't want my people harmed, even if they are storming my castle. Use weapons if you like, but make sure they're weapons that won't hurt anyone."

"As you wish, Your Majesty!" said Centurion Alisha, and she and the guards thundered down the stone stairs to the weapons storeroom. They found the cupboard marked WEAPONS THAT WON'T HURT ANYONE and pulled out lots of inflatable hammers.

The guards ran through the castle,
doing their best—but the inflatable hammers
didn't scare anyone. They just bounced
harmlessly off every peasant head.

King Edwin, Minister Jill, and Megan the Jester watched it all from the battlements.

"The castle is lost! Your Majesty, we must flee!" said Minister Jill.

There aren't many ways into a castle, which is a problem when you want to get out of one because there aren't many ways to do that, either. Edwin ran to the weapons storeroom to see if anything was there that might help.

He found a bow and arrow.

The king scurried back up to the battlements, tied some string to the arrow, and fired it over the moat. The arrow stuck in a tree on the other side, trailing the string

behind it, which Edwin

caught and tied to a

stone pillar.

"Okay. All we need to do now is
tightrope-walk over the castle moat that's
totally full of crocodiles,
and we'll be safe on
the other side."
"Ever walked on a
tightrope before?" said Minister Jill.
"Uuuummmmmmmmmmm . . . no,"
said King Edwin.

6.

Snappy Crocodiles

"I'll go first to check it's safe," said Minister Jill, trying to sound as brave as she could.

The string wobbled as she took the first few steps over the moat.

Far below, crocodiles snapped and

wriggled in the water, expecting a meal to plop into their mouths any second. A couple of years before, King Edwin had crocodiles put in the moat because he thought crocodiles were awesome. Didn't seem like such a good idea now.

But Jill took a deep breath, kept walking, and jumped to safety on the other side.

Megan the Jester went next. The crocodiles snapped and drooled. This would be a really, *really* big meal for them. They might have to eat a few tinkly bells as they gobbled her up, but they could pick those out of their teeth later.

Megan fell over a lot to make the king

laugh. But when she did that, she was trying

to walk in a straight line. That's what made it funny.

"Megan!" shouted Edwin. "Just try really hard to fall off the string, and then you're bound to stay on!"

She did what he said, and she instantly became an expert tightrope walker. She stood on one leg, she balanced on one toe, she walked in a perfect straight line, all with her eyes closed. It was impossible for her to fall off.

The crocodiles were furious.

Megan reached the end of the string and jumped onto the grass.

King Edwin went last. *Don't think about the crocodiles' teeth*, he thought to himself. *Forget all about those shiny, sharp, terrifying teeth. Also don't get distracted by thinking about all the nice animals you could have put*

in the moat instead of crocodiles, like ducks

or swans or—

He shook, he wobbled, and his beloved
crown fell off his head.

*No **no no!*** he thought. *What's a king without his crown?*

So he stepped off the string . . .

grabbed the crown in midair . . .

then fell . . .

and grabbed the string with his little finger.

"I'm perfectly fine!" he shouted to the other two, who could barely watch.

If you had grabbed that rope with just a little finger, you'd have fallen and gotten yourself munched by crocodiles. Luckily King Edwin did little-finger exercises every day, so his finger was really muscly.

He clambered back onto the string.

"See, I knew exactly what I was doing," he fibbed as he jumped to the ground next to his friends.

As the three of them ran away over the hills, King Edwin looked back and saw the flag of Emperor Nurbison raised over the castle. You might think that an evil emperor's flag would have snakes or wolves on it, but Nurbison's didn't.

That night, hiding on the misty mountain of Hetherang-Dundister-Underploshy-Smeltus, which hardly anyone visits because it's so hard to ask the way there, Minister Jill lit a match. She, King Edwin, and Megan the Jester sat around it, trying to keep warm.

They were all pretty miserable, as you would be if you'd just been kicked out of your own kingdom.

"Shall I do another song?" said Megan.

"Yeah, that might cheer us up." said Edwin.

Megan the Jester pulled her backup lute out of a special pocket in her hat and sang.

Stick your toes
Up your nose.
Everybody, stick your toes
Up your nose.

Stick your toes
Up your nose.
You gotta stick your toes
Right up your nose.

The song went on like this for quite a while. They all did the actions. But even

something as fun as sticking toes up noses couldn't lift the gloom they felt.

Minister Jill wasn't just sad—she was frightened. She didn't like danger. That's why she had a desk job in the castle.

"We'll never be safe from Emperor Nurbison, even up here," she said. "There's nothing else to do. We'll have to flee. Somewhere he'll never find us."

"I can't do that! I love my kingdom," said King Edwin. "I could never love another land nearly as much."

"There are loads of other lands in the world," said Minister Jill. "There must be at least one you'd enjoy."

"Like where?" asked the king.

"There's Gray Cardigan Land. They say it's incredible. Some of the cardigans are so amazingly, dazzlingly gray that it hurts your eyes to look at them."

Minister Jill had always wanted to go to Gray Cardigan Land, but the king didn't think it sounded very interesting. He shook his head.

"Vegetable Eating Land? You're sure to love that."

King Edwin wasn't sure at all.

"Homework Land? The Land of Never-Ending Drizzle?"

King Edwin shook his head.

"Ah! Theme Park Land!" said Minister

Jill. "Everyone eats cotton candy for breakfast, lunch, and dinner; travels everywhere by roller coasters; and rides a log flume instead of having a bath."

King Edwin decided that, yes, Theme Park Land did sound kind of okay.

The three friends crept down the mountain to the shore. Minister Jill kept a secret rowing boat in a little bay, just in case of emergencies. A few moments later, the boat was cutting through the waves, the strong arms of Megan the Jester heaving the paddle.

"Theme Park Land, here we come!" said Megan.

King Edwin stood up in the boat.

"No! I just can't do it! I can't leave my kingdom!" he said. "I'll find a way to win it back. Who's with me?"

The Rules

Centurion Alisha and the palace guards battled on bravely until dawn. But one by one, their inflatable hammers were burst by the peasants' pitchforks and the pointy axes of Emperor Nurbison's sinister soldiers.

"SEIZE THEM!" bellowed Emperor Nurbison, who had been dying to say that for hours. The palace guards were tied up

with string from the emperor's crafting box.

The people of Edwinland
gathered in front of
the castle, waiting
to find out about
all the great
things that would
happen now that
Emperor Nurbison
was in charge.

This time,
there was no
hay cart
handy for
the emperor
to speak
from, so

Globulus ordered lots of peasants to lie on the ground. Then he told more peasants to lie on top of them, then more peasants on top of those. Soon there was a mound of peasants as tall as an elephant, with arms and legs sticking out all over the place.

Before the emperor climbed to the top, he took off his spiky-heeled boots.

Then he put on some even spikier-heeled ones.

The hill said things like **"oof!"** and

"ouch!" as Emperor Nurbison marched to

the summit.

Some of the peasants started to worry that

something wasn't quite right about all this.

"Subjects!" said Emperor Nurbison. "King

Edwin is gone forever. You are now servants

of Emperor Nurbison! Globulus, tell them the

new rules."

- **CHOCOLATE** is banned
- And **MUSIC**
- And **DANCING**
- And **SPORTS**
- And **FUN OF ANY KIND**
- Everyone must dress in **DIRTY RAGS**
- Every day of the week is now **MONDAY** so it will be **MONDAY FOREVER**
- Anyone who thinks a bad thought about the emperor will spend **3 HOURS** in a **BATH OF SPIDERS**
- Edwin's palace guards will be locked away so **THEY WON'T SAVE YOU**
- And any other nasty things that the emperor has forgotten right now will become rules just as soon as he thinks of them

The crowd, who were now pretty sure they had made a mistake, groaned as Globulus announced each rule.

As the peasants tried to get their heads around all that, a sinister soldier handed the emperor a flaming torch.

The emperor hurled the torch. It landed on K.E.N.N.E.T.H.

Soon, all the pipes and springs and twirly cogs of K.E.N.N.E.T.H. were blazing.

"Yes! You have all been fooled! By me!" cackled Emperor Nurbison. "And when at last I find where King Edwin is hiding, my revenge shall be complete!"

The emperor swirled his cloak and set off back to his evil castle with a last bloodcurdling

"FOO HOO HOO HOO."

The peasants were puzzled.

"That's his evil laugh!" said Globulus.

"Be afraid, peasants!"

The peasants were afraid.

Sneaky Plan

King Edwin, Minister Jill, and Megan the Jester
were hiding high on a mountain, up a tree.

It was a very small tree. It didn't hide
much more than Minister Jill's head, King
Edwin's feet, and Megan's bum. Megan was
so big and heavy that the tree bent over and
was almost touching the ground. But there

aren't many trees at all on the slopes of Hetherang-Dundister-Underploshy-Smeltus, so they didn't have a lot of choice.

"We need a sneaky plan to defeat evil Emperor Nurbison," said King Edwin. "I don't know if I can think one up because I've never had a sneaky plan in my life."

Minister Jill knew this wasn't quite true. When the king was younger, there was one night when every single chocolate cookie in the castle disappeared. The next morning, Edwin said he didn't know what happened, even though he had chocolate smeared all around his mouth. Because he was the king, nobody said anything more about it.

Honestly, kings have it easy sometimes, thought Jill.

"I've got it!" said the king. "He tricked the peasants by disguising a cow. If we disguise *ourselves*, maybe we can trick *him*. The first thing is to get out of this tree."

Megan got out of the tree first. The tree *twang*ed back up. Minister Jill and King Edwin were catapulted into a pond.

"The second thing," said King Edwin, once he had banged the tadpoles out of his ear, "is  to get out of this pond and into the empire of Nurbisonia."

They walked down the mountain, across the dotted white line, and into enemy territory.

The third thing was to dress like Nurbisonian peasants. Because all the peasants in Nurbison's empire wore dirty rags, this wasn't too hard to do. They dragged their clothes through thorny brambles, then splattered them

with mud and rabbit poo, and soon they had
three authentic, stinking peasant outfits.

They looked absolutely, exactly like
peasants. Except Megan was wearing a jingling
jester hat, and Minister Jill still had her badge.

So Jill stuffed her badge and Megan's hat
into a hedge.

She reached for King Edwin's crown.
But he stepped away.

"No, not that!" said King Edwin. "I have to keep wearing it. What's a king without his crown?"

So the crown needed its own disguise. Megan ran around a field until she caught two straggly sheep—one black, one white. Minister Jill shaved them with a sharpened flint and wove a colossal black-and-white wig for Edwin to wear.

Edwin's new hair was bigger than he
was. But at least you couldn't see the crown.

Now they were ready.

They walked deep into Nurbisonia. It
wasn't like home. Trees were twistier, with
no leaves. They heard the spooky sound of
howling wind. They figured out it was
coming from a peasant who was making the
sound with his mouth, but it was spooky
all the same.

On the horizon they saw the emperor's
thin castle, cloaked by a swirl of lightning-
spitting clouds. That was the place to go.

It was a long walk. Edwin had now been one whole day, one whole night, and a bit more of a day without chocolate. His legs felt wobbly. Boys and girls need chocolate like they need air.

Outside the evil castle, it wasn't too hard to find Emperor Nurbison. He was riding round and round in a chariot pulled by all the pets from King Edwin's kingdom.

There were twenty-three cats, fifteen dogs, some horses, some goats, a pig, two lizards, a goldfish, and a stick insect. The stick insect

was pulling harder than all the other animals put together, mostly because the lizards were trying to eat it. The emperor's sinister soldiers ran alongside, saying nice things about the emperor's driving, just like they'd been told to, while the chariot ran over their feet.

"We must save the animals!" said Jill.

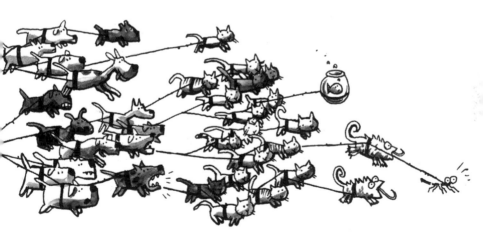

"That'll have to wait," said King Edwin. "Right now, you have to find a massive lump of mud and throw it at the emperor's face."

"What? Why?" said Minister Jill.

"If I told you my whole plan at the start, that would be a lot less fun," said King Edwin.

Soon Minister Jill was hiding behind a rock with a HUGE lump of mud. King Edwin and Megan the Jester crouched in a field close by, plowing the earth with their bare hands, because that's a very peasanty thing to do. But all the time they were really looking at the road.

"Here comes the chariot again! Get ready!" shouted the king.

As Emperor Nurbison rumbled into view, Minister Jill threw the mud with all her might. It hurtled straight toward the emperor's head.

Megan the Jester picked up King Edwin by the ankles and hurled him. Hard. Just before the lump hit the emperor's face, King Edwin caught it in midair.

"CEASE!" said Emperor Nurbison.

The panting animals came to a stop. King Edwin splashed into a puddle by the road, still clutching the mud.

"Soldiers! You have failed me!" said the emperor. "That foul lump of soil was about to strike my stunningly handsome face, and you did nothing to stop it. Nothing! Only this small peasant boy with massive black-and-white hair could save me from filthiness. How shall I reward this miserable wretch? One more rotten carrot this week? Maybe some extra work. Peasants love work."

"My lord," said King Edwin, "may I become one of your sinister soldiers? With my two friends here?"

Megan the Jester and Minister Jill stepped forward. The emperor twiddled his diabolical beard as he thought.

"Well, you saved my face once. Perhaps you could do it again. But . . ."

The emperor peered hard into King Edwin's eyes.

"You have peculiar hair for a peasant. So much of it. You look almost like a sheep. Very unusual. There's nothing else going on here, is there?"

Jill and Megan did a joint gulp.

"No. No. **Nonononono.** And no," said King Edwin.

"Then I've decided," said the emperor. "All three of you shall join the sinister soldiers. Open my castle gates! Let them in!"

← (SHAVED SHEEP)

9.

The Room of Temptation

They didn't become sinister soldiers right away. They had to pass some tests.

The first one wasn't too hard. It was a multiple-choice quiz, with questions like

Q: WHO IS THE MOST AMAZING PERSON IN THE UNIVERSE?

A) Somebody who just won a school art competition

B) Your granddad, who can pull a coin from behind your ear

C) The astonishing, stunning, awesome, and breathtaking master of all the earth, Emperor Nurbison, whose very words command the sun, moon, and stars

D) Your cousin, who can make the noise with his armpit that his mom doesn't like

They were all very careful to put down C for that one. Even Megan, whose granddad could do the coin thing *and* pretend to grab her nose with his fingers.

The second test was much tougher.

"Edwin the so-called king still hasn't

been found," said Emperor Nurbison, "so he

might be in these lands, in an incredibly good disguise. We all know how much he likes chocolate. So I'm going to put you all in this room full of chocolate. If one of you eats even a tiny scrap of chocolate, I'll know you are really King Edwin. Clever, eh?"

So, King Edwin, Minister Jill, and Megan the Jester were locked in a

big room in Nurbison's castle. It was piled

high with the tastiest treats you can imagine.

Chocolate-smothered cookies with

that layer of minty stuff inside. Triangular

chocolate. Nutty chocolate. Chocolate

wafers, chocolate bars, chocolate

oranges, and, best of all, chocolates

that had been coated with

chocolate, dipped in

chocolate, sprinkled

with chocolate, and then put in a box made of chocolate, too. Which was tied with a ribbon made of chocolate.

Edwin hadn't seen anything like this for two whole days, and he was dying to cram the whole lot in his mouth.

He sweated and twitched.

It would be soooooo good to eat just a tiny bit.

Edwin's shaking hand reached out to break the corner off a big hazelnut bar. Nobody would notice a teensy weensy bit of a corner, surely. . . .

But if they did, he'd be discovered and his kingdom would never be free. So he pulled his hand back and sat calmly, as if chocolate meant nothing to him.

A few hours later, the door was unlocked. They were given uniforms. Megan, Jill, and Edwin were sinister soldiers.

• • •

Now that he had added Edwin's kingdom to his own, Emperor Nurbison was feeling quite pleased with himself. He summoned Globulus by

BwwwoOOooOoNNNGgggGGGg

whacking a massive gong the size of a kiddie pool.

"Globulus! I demand a feast," the emperor said to Globulus. At least, he was pretty sure it was Globulus. It was hard for the emperor to see because the ringing gong was still making his eyes vibrate in his head.

"So, like, ah, you know, a really big one, my lord?" said Globulus.

The emperor sighed. What a stupid question. Who ever heard of a tiny feast? *Maybe I should find some clever people to hang around this castle instead of Globulus*, he thought. Then he realized that clever people might not agree with him all the time. So Globulus could stay.

"Yes, of course a big feast," the emperor said. "I'm an emperor, so it's got to be a massive feast. A ginormous feast, with guests. Summon all the rulers of all the evil kingdoms in the world!"

The invitations were sent out by peasant post. That's where you get a peasant to remember a message, something like "Come to Emperor Nurbison's castle on Wednesday," then you write an address on the peasant, stick a stamp on his head, and ram him into a mailbox. When the peasant is delivered to the right address, he speaks the message out loud. It works ever so well.

From far and wide the evil rulers came.

First came . . .

THE POTENTATE OF QUIVE.

Then . . .

THE ARCH MANDRAKE OF CLAB

WIDE HEAD MEANS ROOM FOR 3 CROWNS

and the . . .

KARZI OF ELAM.

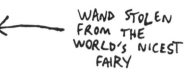

WAND STOLEN
FROM THE
WORLD'S NICEST
FAIRY

Then came . . .

DUKE UMBRAGE OF ICKUM BOKUM

Then came . . .

HIGH WARRIOR UNTH-GUNTH OF THE NORTHERN NORTHLANDS TO THE NORTH,

MAMMOTH-SKIN HAT

MAMMOTH-SKIN UNDERPANTS

YEP, MORE MAMMOTH

and . . .

SUPREME WITCH
HULLISTIA OF
THE SOUTHERN
SOUTHLANDS
TO THE SOUTH.

Loads of them came. Hundreds. Outside

the emperor's castle there was a three-mile-

long traffic jam of evil stagecoaches.

Luckily, the emperor's place had hundreds of spare bedrooms for them. The Arch Mandrake of Clab, the fattest of all the guests, was put in a room in the very spindliest tower. It snapped off and tumbled into the bottomless pit, taking the Arch Mandrake with it. The other rulers didn't mind too much. He wasn't exactly evil anyway—just a bit annoying.

(THE LAST ANYONE HEARD OF THE ARCH MANDRAKE OF CLAB)

In a dark corner of the castle, three sinister soldiers shuffled close together. It was Megan the Jester, Minister Jill, and King Edwin.

"I've been standing around looking sinister for days," said Megan. "Do you know how hard that is for a jester?"

"Bet you're wondering what my next plan is," said King Edwin.

"Yes, I think I'd like to know a bit beforehand this time," said Minister Jill.

King Edwin told them everything.

"The feast will be tonight. The sinister soldiers will work as waiters. I'll volunteer to be the emperor's personal lemonade pourer. I'll just keep filling his lemonade glass over and over, until he drinks so much he needs a very long pee. I'll bet he'll say something like 'I need a very long pee now,' so nobody will expect him back for a while. You two will guard the corridor on the way to the bathroom. You'll grab him and get him out of the castle. Once he's our prisoner, we won't let him go until he gives us our kingdom back! What do you think?"

Minister Jill could see a problem.

"What about you, my king?" she said.

"You'll be trapped in a room full of the most evil people on earth. How will you escape?"

"Oh, I don't know. I suppose I'll just jump on a horse or something," said King Edwin, who really hadn't thought that far ahead.

10.

We Feast!

Globulus banged the giant gong. It vibrated so much that two fillings fell out of his teeth.

"It's, you know, kind of, like, dinnertime? For the evil rulers of the world and all that and everything?" announced Globulus.

That meant it was dinnertime for the evil rulers of the world.

They walked into the great hall of
Nurbison's castle, glittering in all the crazy
outfits they had designed for the feast.

Countess Crakey had a dress made out of
living snakes.

Duke Umbrage had awarded himself so
many medals that he ran out of space on his
own body and needed another three people
walking behind him to wear the rest.

CLINK CLANK CLINKETY RATTLE CLINK CLINK

Spion Ratchet wore a suit of armor made out of human toenail clippings. For some reason, nobody wanted to sit next to him.

Emperor Nurbison sat on a big throne above them all, his spiky crown looking spikier than ever, its anti-diamonds not-glittering beautifully. They ate lots of fancy olden-days foods you don't see much now.

GIRAFFE'S NECK ON TOAST

PIG'S HEAD WITH AN APPLE IN THE MOUTH

FRIED WATER

All through the evening, King Edwin poured lemonade for everyone—but especially Emperor Nurbison.

At last—hopping from side to side a bit—the emperor stood up to make his big speech.

"CEASE! Diabolically nasty rulers of the world, welcome to my sinister and terrifying castle. I have brought you here to celebrate my takeover of Edwinland. I crushed it as easily as you crush that fruit. Go on, everybody! Crush a fruit!

FOO HOO HOO HOO!"

Nice soft fruits like strawberries and peeled bananas had been put in front of all the evil rulers. They cackled away as they crushed.

What a fun party this was—if you were
massively wicked.

"Yet my victory is not complete, for King
Edwin has still not been found! Curse that child!"

The party guests gave loud boos for
King Edwin.

Emperor Nurbison looked more and more
uncomfortable. The lemonade was working!

"But now, dear friends, I must cut my speech short because . . ."

This was the moment. King Edwin stood ready to guide the emperor down the corridor to the bathroom, where Jill and Megan were waiting.

"Because I have to say—guards . . .

Hundreds of sinister soldiers burst through the hall's main door and grabbed King Edwin.

More guards burst through another door, holding Minister Jill and Megan the Jester. Lots of doors, lots of bursting, lots of soldiers.

Emperor Nurbison grinned at his captives.

"Do you really think you had me fooled for a moment, with that ridiculous sheep's hair?" said the emperor, snatching off King Edwin's

giant wool wig. There was Edwin's gleaming crown for all to see.

The emperor grabbed the crown and threw it to Globulus, who dropped it into a treasure chest and locked the lid.

"No, I knew it was you all along," the emperor said. "But I let you join my soldiers so I could have the pure pleasure of unmasking you here, before the most evil people in the world! What do you think of that, King Flashypants?"

The horribly wicked crowd roared and cackled. Edwin, Jill, and Megan were very brave about it all. Except Megan, who completely wasn't.

King Edwin's heart was broken. He knew

he would never see his crown again. Or see his castle again. And his people would never be free.

And he'd never taste chocolate again.

NEVER TASTE CHOCOLATE AGAIN.

He *really* needed to think of a plan now.

"And now, you foolish fools, I will give you a choice," said Emperor Nurbison. "You may either spend the rest of your days chained to the wall in my dungeon. Or . . ."

King Edwin saw Megan smiling. Oh dear. Megan probably thought the other choice would be something nice, like a puppet show or a sports day with obstacle races and a raffle.

"Or," the emperor said, "you will be thrown off my castle into the bottomless pit, to fall forever. Choose!"

Falling was Megan's favorite thing to do. But she also liked getting up again afterward, and you can't do that if you're falling forever.

Megan took a deep breath. She was about to say "dungeon."

Minister Jill opened her mouth. She was about to say "dungeon."

King Edwin was moving his tongue around his cheek in the way he did just before he had a really *big* idea.

"Decide!" spat Emperor Nurbison.

"Bottomless pit," said King Edwin.

"Your king has decided for you," said the emperor. "You will all be thrown off the castle. I will push you over myself. And now . . ."

The emperor did his most serious voice.

"Now I have to go and do a really, really
long pee."

11.

The Bottomless Pit

The next morning, Emperor Nurbison led his three prisoners and all the nastiest rulers of the world up to the highest tower of his palace. It was so high that the birds crackled as they flew because their wings kept icing up from the cold.

The
sinister soldiers
prodded King
Edwin, Megan the
Jester, and Minister Jill
with their pointy spears.

"Your Majesty," whispered
Minister Jill, "do you have some kind of
plan to get us out of this? Because
it would be really, really good if you do."

"There's a plan, all right," King Edwin
whispered back. "And it's going to work fine so
long as they don't tie our hands. That would
mess everything up."

"TIE THEIR HANDS!" shouted the emperor.

The evil soldiers tied the prisoners' hands behind their backs with thicker string than they'd used on Edwin's palace guards. It was so thick, it was like rope. In fact, it was rope.

This was a very bad situation.

The evil rulers laughed—except the ones whose noses had filled up with ice. They made a kind of snorty, splintering sound.

King Edwin peered over the edge.

Far below were swirling mists and a hole where he and his friends would fall forever and ever.

And ever.

And ever.

And ever.

You could keep saying "and ever" as many times as you'd like, and it still wouldn't last for as long as their fall.

Unless somebody could think of something to save the day.

"Sire, I reckon you're meant to, you know, ask them if they have any last requests, that kind of thing," said Globulus.

"Oh, do I have to?" said the emperor. "That's just a bit soppy."

The other rulers mumbled and grumbled. Even really evil people think that if you're going to shove somebody off a castle, you have to give them a final wish.

"Oh, all right then, if I must," said the emperor. "Any last requests?"

"I've got one! I've got one!" said Megan. "I want to *not* be pushed into the hole!"

"Well, I can't grant you that one!" said the emperor. "Obviously! Or nobody would ever get pushed into bottomless pits at all. That's just common sense. Dear me, the jesters you get these days. Anybody else?"

Minister Jill stepped forward.

"King Edwin's request is to scratch his itchy bum," said Minister Jill.

Nobody expected that.

"I don't get it. How do you know if he's got an itchy bum or not?" said Emperor Nurbison.

"It doesn't *feel* all that itchy," King Edwin said.

"Yes, it does," said Minister Jill.

"But it's not very itchy at all. In fact, it's very un-itchy," said the king.

"But it really is ever so itchy," said Minister Jill.

"Is the bum itchy or not? Can't the two of you decide?" said the emperor.

"King Edwin," said Minister Jill, "you *do* have an itchy bum, and you *must* scratch it before you fall. If you lean up against that very rough, rocky wall—that one over there that's all covered in very, very sharp flints—you could scratch it."

King Edwin wondered if there was something wrong with Minister Jill's eye. She couldn't stop winking.

Then he thought, *Maybe I should do what she says.*

"Ooo! Ow! I just noticed how incredibly itchy my bum is! Could I scratch it? Please?" said Edwin.

"Go on, then. But make it quick," said the emperor.

King Edwin leaned against the wall and wriggled around. Everyone looked the other way.

"Mmmm. Just need to scratch a bit more," King Edwin said.

"Come on, come on! You've had ages!" said

the emperor.

"Just a moment more. . . . There!" said King Edwin, jumping forward. "Now then, how about I go over first?"

The king perched on the very edge of the battlements, facing Nurbison and the evil crowd. The emperor's great twisted crown vibrated in the wind, its anti-diamonds catching and keeping the rays of the rising sun.

Emperor Nurbison was about to push King Edwin into the bottomless pit.

"I'm about to push you into the bottomless pit," said the emperor.

Everybody held their breath.

And, just as the emperor was about to shove the king over . . .

King Edwin snatched Emperor Nurbison's crown right from his head.

All the evil rulers gasped.

The king dangled it over the castle's edge.

"B-but how? They tied you up!" spluttered the emperor.

"I wasn't really scratching my bum!" said King Edwin. "I was cutting through the rope on a spiky rock on your spiky castle! And now, Emperor Nurbison, I have your oh-so-valuable crown hanging over the edge of this bottomless pit. Push me over, and your crown goes with me. And what's a king—or an emperor— without his crown?"

Emperor Nurbison boiled inside. The horrible boy had outwitted him. He wanted to shove the brat over the edge there and then, but that would mean losing his crown forever in front of all these evil men and women, and they would never stop laughing about it behind his back. You just can't trust evil people to say nice things about you when you're not there.

"That crown is priceless! It's worth one hundred times what your crown's worth! Despicable tot! Loathsome infant! Vile minor! Appalling juvenile! Hateful youngster!"

The emperor carried on for a bit like this,

until he'd used up all the words he knew meaning "horrible" and "child."

"What will it take?" said the emperor. "What will it take for you to give me back my beloved crown?"

"Easy," said King Edwin. "All you have to do is let my friends go home—and all the pets, give me back *my* crown, and set my kingdom free."

"Well, you seem to have thought of *everything*," said the emperor, smiling.

Minister Jill glared at King Edwin as if she was trying to tell him something.

Edwin became very worried.

Was there something else?

Yes, there was.

"Oh yeah! And you have to let me go home as well and not push me into a bottomless pit, where I will fall forever. That, too. That's quite important. So, do we have a deal?"

Emperor Nurbison looked at the evil rulers. Some of the men were twirling mustaches in amusement. Some of the women, too. Others sniggered and chortled behind their hands.

All of them were laughing at him, the evil emperor, who had been tricked by a child.

"Emperor? What do you say?" asked King Edwin.

"I say . . . I say . . ."

The emperor's knuckles wriggled under his skin.

"All right, yes! We have a deal!"

What We've All Learned

Whenever King Edwin and his subjects had an adventure, they would get together on the village green afterward to talk about what they'd all learned. So, after Emperor Nurbison's soldiers had been booted out of the kingdom, and Minister Jill, Megan the Jester, and King Edwin had returned home (along with all the pets), and the emperor had gotten his crown back, and Uncle Gavin's treasure boat *finally* arrived with Edwin's birthday money, that's just what they did.

One of the peasants stood up.

"We peasants have learned something. We've learned to be more patient, and to not turn against our king just because he hasn't given us free chocolate on a Friday."

Everybody cheered. Then

Minister Jill stood up.

I'VE LEARNED JUST HOW BRAVE AND CLEVER OUR KING IS!

said the

minister, who had also

learned how her king could

put her in lots of frightening

situations. But she decided not to

mention that part.

"I learned something," said Megan the Jester. Everybody waited for her to finish. She was sure she had learned something, something very special and wise, but she couldn't work out exactly what it was. So in the end she just sat down again.

King Edwin stood up. "I've certainly

learned something. I've learned that it was

me not taking care of my own money that got us into the whole mess. And that's why I've decided to let Minister Jill look after the pocket money from now on."

Minister Jill wasn't too happy to hear this. It meant more work for her.

"I've also learned that Minister Jill and Megan the Jester are the best, most loyal friends in the whole world," said the king, and everybody shouted, "Hooray!"

Minister Jill felt much happier.

"Also, I've decided to change my name from King Edwin to **KING EDWIN FLASHYPANTS**. I know the emperor said it to tease me, but I sort of like the sound of it." And with that, King Edwin Flashypants sat down.

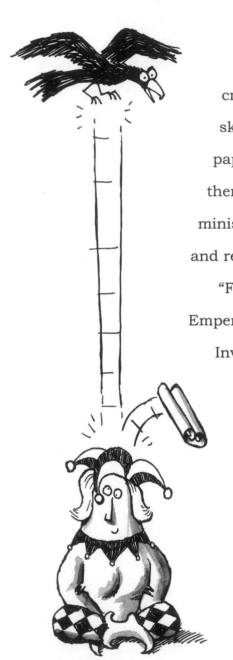

A single black crow flapped across the sky, dropped a scroll of paper onto Megan's head, then flapped away. The minister unrolled the paper and read.

"From His Majesty Emperor Nurbison of the Invincible Empire of Nurbisonia, Earl of Unjerland, Overlord of . . ." Jill decided to skip to the end. "I've learned something, too, you unworthy vermin. I've learned I'll have to become even more evil to defeat you.

Do you hear me? Even more evil!

FOO HOO HOO HOO HOO!"

But nobody really cared what Nurbison thought.

Now that all the learning had been done, it was time to celebrate. A brass band played a well-known tune called "Edwin Is a Fantastic King, He's Just the Best, Yes He Is, and If You Don't Think So, You're Just a Wrongy Wrong-Face."

King Edwin threw great handfuls of chocolate into the crowd and ran around high-fiving everyone.

"There's just one thing I don't get," said Minister Jill to a nearby group of peasants. "Why did you think that a cow with candles on its nose was a dragon?"

"Oh, it was an amazing disguise, that.

Nobody could tell it was just a cow," said one peasant.

"I did! I always said it was a cow!" said Natasha, the little girl.

"Like I said, not one of us saw it was a cow," said the peasant. "Because if someone had, and they said it and we didn't believe them, the rest of us would feel really embarrassed now, wouldn't we?"

"But I *did* say it was a cow! I did!" said Natasha.

Then Natasha was given some extra chocolate by her mom and dad to keep her quiet in front of the minister, and everybody was happy.

The fun in Village carried on all afternoon and into the night. There was karaoke, a tin-tray-bashing competition, and an orchestra of honky horns. Megan the Jester had the whole party sticking their toes up their noses. Things got pretty loud.

The sound carried far, far away, beyond Edwinland, over the Plains of Yerm, and into the Wilderness of Crong.

There, in a dark cave, the noise
stirred a sleeping shape.

It awoke.

It opened one eye.

Then it opened

another eye.

And another eye.

And another.

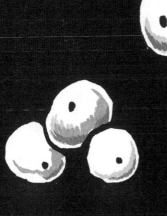

And another
after that.

And then a load more eyes.

Then—oh yes,
some more eyes.

Then some more.

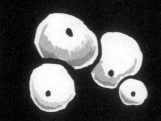

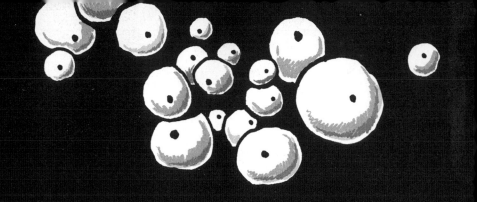

What kind of

BEAST

had awoken?

We will find out.

In another book.

The End

THE EMPEROR'S STRIDING THEME

THE EMPEROR'S STRIDING THEME

CHORDS FOR
PLAYING ALONG
ON GUITAR OR
PIANO OR LUTE

TEMPO: STRIDING SPEED

Emp - er - or   Nur - bi - son,

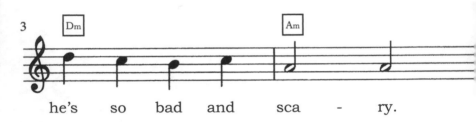

he's   so   bad   and   sca   -   ry.

Ask   his   mom   if   he's   fun,

she'll   say,   "No,   not   ve   -   ry."

ANDY RILEY has done lots of funny writing for film and TV, and he's even won prizes for it, like BAFTAs and an Emmy. For TV, Andy cowrote the scripts for David Walliams's *Gangsta Granny* and *The Boy in the Dress*, and *Robbie the Reindeer*. The films he's written for include *Gnomeo and Juliet* and *The Pirates! In an Adventure with Scientists!* Andy really loves cowboy hats, and he can do a brilliant "FOO HOO HOO."